Tara and her Talking Kitten Meet a Mermaid

This book is dedicated to my grandchildren
Isabel, Finn, Kailani, Maya and Taliya
and children everywhere who love kittens.

Discussion points and exercises for children are on pages 78–79.

Diana Cooper is well known for her books on angels, fairies, unicorns and the spiritual world, all written from her own personal experiences. For more information about these subjects see her website www.dianacooper.com *– there is also a children's corner.*

If you wish to talk to someone about the subjects in this book, the Diana Cooper School website lists teachers throughout the world: www.dianacooperschool.com

Text © Diana Cooper 2012
Edited by Nicky Leach
Illustrations © Kate Shannon 2012
Interior design by Thierry Bogliolo

ISBN 978-1-84409-580-3

Printed in the European Union

Published by
Findhorn Press
117–121 High Street
Forres IV36 1PA
Scotland, UK

www.findhornpress.com

Tara and
her Talking Kitten
Meet a Mermaid

by Diana Cooper
illustrated by Kate Shannon

FINDHORN PRESS

A Fairy Visits Tara

It was the weekend. Tara was sitting at the kitchen table doing her spelling homework. She felt grumpy because she didn't think you should have homework when you were seven years old and she knew Ash-ting her kitten agreed with her. He was soft, grey, and fluffy, and they could talk to each other. But nobody knew!

Suddenly they heard a quiet tapping.

"Perhaps it's Mummy upstairs," said Tara.

"No, it's outside," replied Ash-ting. *"Someone's at the back door."*

Tara ran to the door and opened it, letting in a blast of cold air. There stood Marigold, a fairy who lived in their garden, looking excited.

She burst out, "The unicorn wants to see you, Tara. He's got a mission for you!"

Unicorns are magnificent pure white horses that most people cannot see, just like they can't see angels or fairies. They have horns of pure white light, and they help the world.

Tara's cross feeling dissolved, and she felt suddenly thrilled.

"What's a mission?" she asked.

"It's a special job!" said Marigold.

"A job for the unicorn!" Tara exclaimed in amazement, for she had met the unicorn before and knew how special they are.

"Yes!" shouted the fairy. "Can you come to the oak tree now?"

In the field at the end of their garden stood a huge oak tree where Tara often played with fairies, elves, imps, and many other elementals.

The little girl looked at Ash-ting, who nodded and said, "Yes, let's go."

So Tara called up the stairs, "Mummy, I've learnt my spelling. Please can I play at the oak tree?"

"Alright, if you are sure you know your words, but just for an hour. It gets cold and dark early."

"Right-o, Mum!"

The child pulled on her coat and boots quickly, hoping that neither her little brother Jack nor her sister Mel would want to join her. She skipped eagerly down the garden path behind the fairy, and Ash-ting ran after them, his tail in the air.

A Mission for Tara

Under the oak tree, dozens of elementals were talking in excited whispers.

"The unicorn came for Tara!" the wee fairy Silver exclaimed.

"It's something important," added an elf. "And. . ."

He fell silent as Tara and Ash-ting arrived with Marigold. Then the little creatures surrounded them, all talking at once.

Suddenly, a dazzling white light approached. Out of it stepped a shimmering unicorn. From his horn he radiated a shower of stars over them, and their auras all lit up.

"Ah, Tara and Ash-ting. Thank you for responding to the call for help."

He tossed his mane with pleasure, then bent his head down so that light from his horn shone onto Tara.

"How can we help?" asked Tara, her heart thumping fast.

"The ocean kingdom is in trouble. Humans are doing bad things to the waters, and the sea creatures are very angry. They want to withdraw their cooperation and start to fight. But that is not the way. It needs a pure child to go to them."

Tara was appalled. "I don't think I'm the right child," she responded humbly. "You see, I'm often in trouble. My sister Mel would be better. She's always good. And. . ." She took a breath. "I don't think I can help."

The unicorn replied gently, "You are genuine, Tara, and very brave. Mel can't see or hear us like you can."

Tara swallowed nervously.

"Ask him what he wants you to do," whispered Ash-ting.

So she repeated Ash-ting's words, asking the unicorn, "What do you want me to do?"

"I'll carry you to the ocean. From there the mermaids will take you to meet the sea creatures."

"Mermaids?" queried Tara, her eyes open wide.

"They're water elementals, cousins of your fairies! They look after the seaweed and ocean plants."

"Oh, but Ash-ting doesn't like water. He's a cat, you see," Tara protested. She could not imagine going without him.

"Perhaps it is better if he doesn't come," the unicorn said gently.

But Ash-ting said stoutly, "Of course I'll come with you, Tara, and do what I can."

Tara bent down and stroked him gratefully. Then she said to the unicorn.
"Mummy wants me home in an hour. I mustn't be late."

"Of course not," replied the unicorn gravely.

So rather reluctantly and not feeling very brave, the little girl and the tiny kitten climbed onto the unicorn's back. Marigold and the other elementals waved goodbye and shouted, "Good luck."

They rose in the air and sped high over the village and meadows. Then they saw the sea like blue silk rolled below them. Still they flew on, until they saw a sandy cove in the distance.

Tara Vanishes

Meanwhile, in Oakhurst Village, Rocky Jones and his parents were taking a shortcut from their home to the shops across the meadow behind Tara's house. Rocky saw Tara under the oak tree with her kitten. The boy used to be an unhappy, nasty bully, but all that changed when Tara, Ash-ting, and the unicorn helped him, and Tara became his friend. He used to be frightened of his dad and anxious for his mum, but now everything was much better.

"There's Tara!" he shouted, raising his hand to wave. "Hi, Tara!"

Then a strange thing happened. As Rocky's parents looked up, there was a sudden burst of sunshine and Tara wasn't there any more. There was no one under the oak tree.

"You must have imagined it," said his dad.

Rocky blinked. Then he rubbed his eyes. He knew he'd seen Tara and Ash-ting! He and his parents walked over to the tree, but there was no sign of them. How very strange!

Meeting a Mermaid

The unicorn flew over the world and at last glided down into a bay of pure white sand with rocks on one side. The sea shimmered as blue as the sky.

Tara and Ash-ting slid onto the sand. The kitten meowed at the sea hoping it would move away. "It's roaring like a lion," he whimpered to Tara.

She laughed at him, but Ash-ting reprimanded her. "You should never laugh at anyone's feelings."

"I'm sorry, Ash-ting," she apologised. "But you are always so brave."

She lifted him carefully onto a solid dry rock. Then she pulled off her boots and socks and ran to paddle in the clear, warm water.

Suddenly, she looked up and saw a little girl about her own age sitting on the rocks. She had big blue-green eyes the colour of the sea, blond hair down to her waist, and a shimmering blue-green tail. She was a mermaid.

Tara stared. She blinked. But the mermaid still sat there, grinning mischievously at her.

Tara ran across the rocks to her, calling, "Hello, I'm Tara."

"I'm Petronella," said the mermaid with a smile. "What's that creature?"

Tara stifled a smile. "That's my kitten, Ashting."

Ash-ting was frowning as he picked his way across the rocks. He did not like the sea, and he most definitely did not like being called a creature in that tone of voice.

"You arrived in a flash of light," said Petronella the mermaid, sounding curious. "How did you do that?"

Tara explained about the unicorn and the mission she'd been given to talk to the ocean creatures. "Will the fish come here to the rocks?" she asked.

"Just a minute," responded Petronella and, rising onto her tail, she dived in a huge arc into the waves and vanished.

"Oh!" gasped Tara and Ash-ting at the same time.

But a second later the mermaid reappeared. "Forgot my conch," she explained. She blew into the shell. The sound travelled across the ocean. "That's to call my brothers. They'll know what to do."

Almost immediately, seven identical heads with blond hair, blue-green eyes, and wide smiles bobbed up in front of them.

Petronella introduced the merboys. "These are my brothers: Jolly, Julian, Joseph, John, Jerry, Jimmy, and Jupiter."

They all grinned and waved.

"The sea creatures are waiting for you in the great cavern," Jolly called. "Follow me."

The Magic Bubble

Tara's stomach flipped. She looked at the ocean in alarm. "But I've only got my 50-metre badge, and I can't swim underwater. I don't like getting my face wet very much—and cats are scared of getting wet, too."

"No problem," said one of the merboys with a grin, leaping out of the ocean to sit beside her. "Here's your magic breathing bubble, and we'll make sure you're safe."

He produced what looked like a goldfish bowl with tubes coming out of it.

"Try it on. You can breathe underwater when you use it, and it regulates your temperature."

"But. . . " Tara protested.

She was too late. The merboy popped the bowl over her head. It felt very comfortable.

"And here's one for the animal," he said.

He handed Petronella a tiny bubble for the kitten, but Ash-ting backed away from them. He had been splashed by spray. His ears and tail drooped, and he looked bedraggled and

18

miserable.

Tara's heart went out to him. She thought of all the times he'd helped her to feel good about herself and said softly, "Wait here, Ash-ting. You can communicate with me from here."

But the stout-hearted kitten said he was not going to leave her. He stood still while Jolly the merboy popped the little bubble over his head and a special cat suit over his body. He looked like a cat in a transparent overcoat and Tara tried not to laugh.

They saw a school of dolphins arcing through

the sea towards them followed by two big turtles.

"They've come to collect you for the meeting," whispered Petronella.

"Wow, I've always wanted to swim with dolphins!" replied Tara, excited.

She picked up Ash-ting. Petronella grabbed Tara's hand. Then they all jumped into the sea!

Fairy Magic

Meanwhile, back at the oak tree, the fairies, elves, brownies, pixies, and other elementals were talking with some urgency about what to do. They did not want anyone realizing that Tara and Ash-ting had vanished.

"Rocky's parents might tell Tara's that she wasn't playing at the tree," said a worried Marigold.

"Tara's parents will be concerned and search for her," agreed a pixie.

"We have to do something to stop them," piped up Silver.

To delay things, a mischievous imp jumped down from the tree and untied Mr. Jones' shoelace, so the big man had to bend down to retie it.

Whallee the elf thought it was time for fairy magic, and all the little folk solemnly agreed. They were only allowed to use it in exceptional circumstances, but this was one of those times.

Mrs. Jones was hugging the tree, while Rocky

was staring up into the branches, sure that Tara
must be sitting up there.

At that moment, the fairies danced a magic
circle round the oak so that Rocky and his
parents were frozen in their positions and could
not move.

Swimming with the Sea Creatures

Petronella the mermaid, Tara, and Ash-ting were in a pale green, watery world. They swam in excited loops around the two big turtles, the mermaid pulling along Tara and Ash-ting. The dolphins leapt and splashed around them, and so did the merboys.

Suddenly, Petronella saw her friend Dolphie, a young dolphin. "Hi, Dolphie," she called, waving with both hands and letting go of Tara, who started to float away.

Jolly saw it and raced after her, grabbing her legs to pull her back. The old turtle grunted that Petronella was irresponsible, but Jolly defended her. He said that Petronella was lots of fun, and he and his brother merboys would teach Tara and Ash-ting to use their legs properly, so that they could move in any direction they wanted to.

Petronella introduced Dolphie to Tara. The young dolphin said that Tara could hold his fin and he would pull her.

"Oh, thank you," Tara gasped in delight and grabbed his fin, still clutching her kitten.

"Race you, Dolphie," yelled Petronella.

"Whee!" shrieked Tara, as Dolphie zipped through the water.

"Meeeeeeooooow," yelled Ash-ting.

It was exhilarating. Dolphie and Petronella were neck and neck. Then Dolphie stopped, and

Tara looked back to see the turtles trailing behind with the merboys.

"It's always great being with you, Petronella," said Dolphie with a smile.

A big dolphin with a wide grin called, "You're a naughty, mischievous, wee mermaid, Petronella, but life's always exciting when you are around."

Petronella laughed. She grabbed Ash-ting and did three backflips. The kitten felt quite dizzy and paddled around in a circle afterwards.

Into the Meeting

Now a huge green curtain of seaweed blocked their way, so they waited for the turtles and merboys to catch up. The dolphins streaked up to them and suggested Tara should sit on one of the giant turtles for it was time to go to the meeting.

Tara's heart skipped a beat at the thought of it, but a big merboy lifted her onto the turtle's back. They placed Ash-ting on the other turtle.

The mermaids pulled back the seaweed. Jolly blew on a conch shell. Then the dolphins led the way, while Tara astride one of the turtles and Ash-ting on the other followed majestically behind them. What a procession!

They entered a vast and beautiful cavern lit up by thousands of lantern fish. As far as she could see millions of sea creatures had gathered. It was an awesome sight.

Whales as big as houses floated at the edges of the crowd. Sharks patrolled each section, keeping order while cheeky little fish nipped across the aisles to see their friends.

All at once, Tara was aware of an enormous, bright aquamarine light. She wondered if Ash-ting could communicate with her when she was underwater.

"Ash-ting, what's the light?" she called to him telepathically.

She felt the familiar buzz in her forehead and was relieved to receive her magical kitten, loud and clear. *The light is Archangel Joules who looks after the oceans,"* said Ash-ting. *"He is watching over the meeting."*

Tara nodded to herself in wonder. She had never seen an archangel before. The light was almost blinding, even though the archangel was at the far end of the cavern.

She noticed that a huge ray floated in front of the shoals of fish. He was clearly in charge of the meeting. As they all made their entrance, the ray greeted them with a wave of his great winglike appendages. Then everyone fell silent.

The Sea Creatures Are Angry

All at once, an angry prawn shouted, "They've polluted our rocks."

A tiny turtle yelled, "Their plastic bags choke us."

A tuna fish grunted, "It's our job to keep the waters of the planet clean and pure, but humans are spoiling it for everyone."

A dolphin added, "Their noise pollution blocks our sonar, so we can't find our way."

One whale grumbled, "They've killed nearly all of us."

A shoal of brightly coloured fish piped up in unison, "They're spoiling our reefs."

And the list of grievances went on and on.

Tara hung her head in shame. People were damaging the seas, the homes of these beautiful intelligent creatures. She felt so sorry for them.

"What have you got to say, human?" called a cod.

"Ash-ting, please help me!" Tara said urgently.

"Show them that you understand," came the response from Ash-ting.

But before Tara could say anything, the unicorn waiting for her above the ocean poured a pure white light down onto them all.

Tara lit up like a beacon. She felt herself getting stronger and braver. All the fish could see the amazing light round her.

She said in a clear voice, "What's happening is terrible. I'm so sorry," and she really meant it. A little ripple of relief passed through the shoals. Someone understood.

"What are you going to do about it?" yelled a haddock.

Tara listened as Ash-ting communicated with her. *"Be honest. Don't promise anything you can't do. Just say that you know that fish and sea creatures are very special and need to be looked after."*

So the little girl told them this, and they all clapped their flippers and fins. She could see their anger was evaporating because one human had understood and been honest.

Then Ash-ting whispered that he had a plan. As he told her his idea, the child's face lit up. "Ash-ting's got an idea about how we'll try to help," she told the gathering. This time they all cheered.

"Who is that creature?" called a tiny sea horse, pointing to Ash-ting.

"It's a catfish," said a barracuda with a laugh, showing a row of sharp teeth. Everyone laughed. But it was friendly laughter, and Ash-ting waved a paw.

A real catfish swam forward then and growled that the creature didn't look in the least bit like him. So Tara told him about her beautiful magical kitten who had wonderful ideas and would find some way of helping all the sea creatures.

The catfish looked happier and swam off with Ash-ting in the direction of the rocks. Tara could hear them chatting together.

A big octopus darted forward and hugged Tara with his eight arms, which quite startled her. All the fish blew bubbles, then they started to leave, swimming back to their own homes.

"Well done, girl," mumbled the old turtle.

A wise dolphin added. "Tara, what you said is important. But it is even more important that you came. Thank you. Now what is Ash-ting's plan?"

But Petronella interrupted by giving her a big hug, saying, "Come on. Let's have some fun! You can tell us about Ash-ting's idea later."

She held Tara's hand and dragged her to a piece of seaweed as thick as a rope. For some time they swung on it together, their hair flying

in the current. Tara felt like Tarzan in the jungle.

Then Petronella spotted a huge old swordfish
asleep under a rock. Quietly, she and Tara swam
up to it and tied his snout up with a piece of
seeweed. Jolly, the biggest merboy, saw this and
told off his naughty sister, but she just laughed!

He offered to carry Tara on his shoulders
back to the rocks. He was very strong, and she
laughed with delight as the merpeople and
Dolphie raced back with them through the waves
to the rocks where Ash-ting and his new friend
the catfish were waiting patiently for her.

The Fairy Spell is Broken

Dad went up to his bedroom to find his glasses. He glanced out the window and was surprised to see Rocky in the meadow staring up into the oak tree. Mr. Jones was bending down to tie his shoelace, and his wife had her arms round the trunk of the tree. He took a second look.

"How very odd," he thought, "and where's Tara?" He decided he had better go and have a look.

As the unicorn arrived back with Tara and Ash-ting, the fairies broke the spell on the Jones family. At the same moment, Dad walked across the field to see what was happening.

They all stared at Tara with their mouths open in astonishment.

"Where have you come from?" Dad asked Tara.

"Nowhere!" said Tara, innocently.

"And what were you all doing?" Dad asked the Joneses, who looked at him puzzled. They had no idea they had been stuck in strange positions all that time.

"Nothing!" they replied in unison.

Tara saw all the wee folk grinning from the branches of the tree and wondered what had been going on.

Mrs Jones stuttered, "Tara, I could have sworn I saw you on a white horse!"

Her dad and Mr. Jones laughed. "You must have imagined it," they said at the same time. Mrs. Jones just nodded perplexed.

Tara hugged Ash-ting close, and Rocky

looked oddly at his friend.

"Ah, well,' said Dad at last, then said to Rocky and his family. "Why don't you come back with us for a cup of tea?"

So they all trooped home to the ordinary warmth of their kitchen. And by bedtime, Tara decided she must have dreamt it all. But as she took off her sock, she found a piece of seaweed stuck to her foot!

The River Floods

That night it rained and rained. All next day, the heavy rain continued.

"I hope the river doesn't burst its banks," commented Dad.

"Oh, do you think the Jones are alright? Their house is right down by the river," replied Mum, sounding concerned.

"I'll phone to check," replied Dad.

He tried their number, and Rocky's father answered. The news was not good. "I'll be right round to help," Dad said, clicking off the phone.

He turned to the family and said, "Bad news. The towpath by the river and the lower part of their garden are flooded. If the river rises much higher, it will get into the house. I'll go there now to help."

Mum said to Dad, "You'll have to take the children. I've got to go to work."

The children had never put on their raincoats and wellingtons so quickly.

Tara gave Ash-ting a quick cuddle. *"Be careful, Tara,"* he warned. Afterwards, she wondered if he knew what was going to happen.

Lots of neighbours had turned out to help. They all remembered how Rocky's Dad had helped the village school build its swimming pool. The men filled bags with sand from Mr. Jones' builder's yard and drove them back on his truck to stack them along the back of the house.

The women and children carried everything they possibly could upstairs in case the water came in. Tara, Mel, and Jack ran up and downstairs, helping willingly.

When everything movable was upstairs, Mrs Bright, Tara's teacher, drove with Tara to the local restaurant and bought piles of fish and chips to feed everyone. Tara was glad to be on her own with Mrs. Bright. Ash-ting had told Tara to talk to Mrs. Bright about all the things humans were doing to the oceans and to ask her to start a petition. *"Children can really help make a difference,"* he had told her.

So now she took the opportunity of telling Mrs. Bright all about the bad things happening to the seas. The teacher heard the passion in Tara's voice and said she would think about the best things to do.

Back at Rocky's house, all the helpers ate fish and chips sitting on the bare floor in the sitting room.

"Just chips for me, please," said Tara.

At last there was a lull in the rain.

"We've done all we can for now. We've run out of sacks to fill with sand," Dad said to the children when they'd finished eating. "Let's go to the bridge and see what the river is doing."

Tara thought about Ash-ting's warning to be careful. She held Dad's hand as they looked down from the bridge at the swirling muddy water racing below them.

A fish came to the surface and flapped its tail at Tara, and she smiled. They watched Mr. Jones stride around the side of his house and paddle down the garden. Rocky was hurrying after him.

"Look, they're saving the rowing boat," Jack shouted, pointing to Rocky's boat, which was tied up where the towpath should have been.

Dad frowned and muttered, "That's dangerous."

Tara felt her stomach clench with fear.

Rocky is Swept Away

Rocky's dad reached the rope that tied the boat to a post. He pulled at it to draw the boat towards him, but it had moved and the back was caught in a bush. They saw him lift his son into the boat and indicate to push it away from the bush with one of the oars while he heaved.

The brown river water was rushing over Mr. Jones's knees, and the boat was rocking. Tara screamed as Rocky's dad slipped and let go of the rope. He disappeared under the water for a moment but surfaced and grabbed the bush that was holding the boat.

The boat lurched as Rocky's dad's weight dislodged it. Then it was carried away by the current into the middle of the racing river with Rocky crouching white-faced in the bottom of the boat.

The boat was swept under the bridge, and they all ran across to watch it, though they hardly dared to look. The boat was completely out of control taken by the current and lurching frighteningly.

They did not see one of the men save Mr.
Jones, who was bellowing for his son.

Tara felt Ash-ting buzz her. The kitten was
psychic, and she knew he was watching from a
distance.

"Call for help," he commanded urgently.

Tara understood he meant her to call on the angels and elementals for assistance. "Help," she screamed loudly. "Help!"

Rocky is Saved

Just ahead of the boat, a huge branch was thrashing in the torrent. Suddenly, an extraordinary thing happened. The branch swerved in front of the boat and seemed to slow it down slightly.

Tara saw Petronella the mermaid's blonde hair swirling in the current as she held the boat. Then she saw that Petronella's merbrothers Jolly, Julian, Joseph, John, Jerry, Jimmy, and Jupiter were pushing the boat towards the river bank to

the place where it sloped gently.

The boat tipped, and Rocky was thrown onto the soggy grass. Tara caught a glimpse of Rocky's guardian angel holding him and sighed with relief. Of course, she was the only one who saw that. Dad, Mel, Jack and the others who had come rushing to the bridge only saw the incredible luck of the branch turning the boat to the bank and tipping the boy out.

Rocky was scrambling up now and running back along the river bank, while his mother was racing towards him holding out her arms to him.

The boat had tipped upside down and was once again caught in the current, floating out of sight. And the rain became a deluge again.

"Rocky was very lucky! That was a miracle!" everyone said in wonder.

Dad said, "Come on. Let's go home now. We've done all we can, and Rocky seems alright."

Tara waved thank you to Petronella and her brothers, and they waved back.

Petronella called, "You have agreed to help the ocean creatures. Now we've helped your friend. Humans and elementals are meant to

work together."

"Hurry up, Tara. Who are you waving to?" asked Dad.

"No one, Daddy," replied Tara.

The Children Help the Oceans

At school the following Monday, Mrs. Bright asked Tara to talk about the oceans and what humans were doing. Tara told such a wonderful story that her teacher said it sounded as if she had been there! Tara just smiled.

The children drew pictures of the ocean. Lots of them drew reefs full of beautiful coral and coloured fish. Some of the boys drew horrible pictures of turtles suffocating on plastic bags and whales being killed. One depicted an oil rig pouring oil into the waters. But Mrs. Bright said all the drawings were perfect.

All the children wrote on their pictures that they wanted to live in a world with clean oceans. Then their teacher gathered them up and sent them to the prime minister through their member of parliament.

That week, Mrs. Bright busied herself phoning everyone she knew. A national newspaper took up the campaign, and children all over the country drew pictures of the ocean world and wrote to their leaders that they wanted to live in a world with clean oceans. Children all over the world did the same thing.

Tara reminded her mum to take a bag when she went shopping so she wouldn't need a plastic one. Rocky reminded his dad to recycle his aluminium beer cans. Tara and Ash-ting sat on the sofa watching a programme on television in which children all over the world were interviewed saying that they wanted clean oceans for the fish and the dolphins and whales. And grownups were listening.

Ash-ting purred. *"I told you, Tara. Children can make a difference. We'd better go to see your friend Petronella again soon to tell her."*

"And your friend, the catfish," said Tara with a grin.

Tara, Ash-ting and the Wallet

Mrs. Pogg Loses Her Wallet

Tara and Ash-ting were looking outof the sitting room window, watching for Daddy coming home.

The little girl stroked her kitten and said, "Daddy's late tonight."

Ash-ting was magic. He and Tara could talk to each other, but no one else knew. He told her about things no one else could see. *"Your daddy has missed his train,"* the kitten murmured.

"Oh," responded Tara, disappointed. "He promised to draw a fairy for me. Now there won't be time." It put her into a bad mood, and she frowned.

Just then old Mrs. Pogg shuffled down the road. She wore a black coat and black hat pulled down against the wind and walked with a stick because of her bad hip. She lived three doors down from Tara.

"Look," said Ash-ting pointing, to distract

Tara from her cross thoughts. *"There's Mrs. Pogg."*

"I don't like her. She's a witch," commented the child rudely.

Ash-ting was patient. *"She's sad and lonely and quite frightened,"* he replied. *"She doesn't have a family round her like you do."*

"Huh," said Tara and shrugged her shoulders.

Just then Mrs. Pogg's wallet slipped from her bag onto the ground. She didn't see it fall, so she limped on.

"Oh no!" exclaimed the little girl.

"Tell your mummy," advised Ash-ting. "Mrs. Pogg can't afford to lose her money."

Tara forgot her bad mood and ran to the kitchen to tell Mummy, but she was on the phone.

"Can't you see I'm busy," her mother shushed her away.

Tara Looks for the Wallet

Tara wasn't supposed to go out onto the pavement on her own, especially when it was getting dark, but this was an emergency.

"Come on, Ash-ting," she said, opening the front door. They latched the door behind them, so that the heat would not escape from inside the house.

It was darker than Tara thought, and she felt rather nervous. The wallet had fallen into the hedge, but she found it at last. Then for the difficult bit—taking it to Mrs. Pogg.

"Perhaps I should just give it to Mummy and let her take it round there?" said Tara.

"No," replied Ash-ting. "Mrs. Pogg will soon realize it is missing, and she'll be very worried."

"Well," Tara swallowed nervously. "Stay right by me, Ash-ting."

They ran to Mrs. Pogg's house before Tara could change her mind. Ash-ting held his tail

straight up in the air.

The little girl's heart thumped at the thought of ringing the old lady's bell. What if she shouted at her?

"Can I ring the bell and leave the wallet on her doorstep?" she asked.

"What would you like if you were elderly and could hardly bend down to pick it up?" the kitten responded quietly.

"For someone to give it to me," Tara replied. She knew she must give the wallet to Mrs. Pogg herself, but she was a bit scared.

Ash-ting nodded. *"Even if it is scary, try to do what you'd like someone to do for you."*

Tara sighed and reached towards the bell, but then a thought struck her. "Perhaps I can push it through the letter box."

Just then she heard a commotion and angry muttering. The door flew open. An angry Mrs. Pogg stood there glaring at them, holding up her stick as if to strike them. She thought they were going to ring the bell and run away.

"You bad child," she shouted. "You think you

can ring my door bell and run away?"

"No," replied the little girl in dismay.

"You just come here," the old lady lurched forward, as if to grab her.

Tara didn't wait. She threw the wallet to Mrs. Pogg, then turned and dashed after Ash-ting, her legs like jelly. They could hear the old lady shouting after them. "Come back, you naughty girl. I saw you. I know who you are. Wait until I tell your parents."

Tara and Ash-ting Hide

Tara could hear Mrs. Pogg hobbling down the road after them. She felt terrified and raced up their front path as fast as she could. Just as she reached their front door, a gust of wind took it and slammed it shut.

"Help," shouted Tara, banging on the door. She could hear Mummy still on the phone. Mrs. Pogg was about to reach their house.

Like lightning, Tara and Ash-ting dived behind a bush. Tara's stomach was clenched, and she felt sick. This was so unfair.

Mrs. Pogg rang their front door bell. She shouted at Mummy when she opened the door: "Where is she? Where have you hidden her? I caught her about to ring my door bell and run away. Then she threw something at me. Let me get my hands on her!"

Mummy looked shocked. Mel and Jack, Tara's brother and sister, appeared from nowhere and stood by her, open mouthed at the sight of

the enraged old lady waving her stick.

"Just a minute, Mrs. Pogg," said Mummy, trying to placate her. "I think there's some mistake. My children are indoors. It must be someone else."

"Where's the dark-haired one, then?" yelled Mrs. Pogg. "It was her."

Mummy called, "Tara, where are you? Come here, please."

There was no reply. How could there be, when Tara was crouching behind the hedge with Ash-ting, horrified at the terrible turn of events. How could her kind deed have gone so wrong?

"Tara, stand up and explain what happened," Ash-ting urged Tara, but the little girl was too scared.

Mummy invited Mrs. Pogg inside while she and Mel and Jack searched for Tara. When they could not find her Mummy was frantic with worry, for it was very dark outside by now.

Mrs. Pogg was triumphant. "I told you so," she said smugly.

Daddy Helps Tara

Outside in the cold and dark Tara shivered, for she had not put on her coat. What was she going to do? She was only trying to be nice, and now she was in trouble. It was so unfair.

Then Ash-ting whispered. *"Your dad's coming. Quick, tell him what happened before he goes indoors."*

So Tara and Ash-ting fled down the road to meet Daddy. Tara ran into his arms and sobbed out the whole story.

"Oh, what a pickle," said Dad, when she had finished. "But it was a kind thought to take the wallet to her, and kind thoughts always work out for the best."

That made Tara feel better. She held Dad's hand tightly as he opened their door and went inside.

Mrs. Pogg was sitting like a big black crow at the kitchen table. "Here she is," she cackled. "The bad girl."

Mummy shrieked, "Tara, where have you

been and what have you done?" She ran towards Tara, as if to shake her.

Daddy held up his hand to stop her. "I think there's been a misunderstanding," he said quietly. "Just listen to Tara's story."

He waited until everyone was silent, then Tara—with a little help from Ash-ting—told them what had really happened.

Mrs. Pogg was deeply embarassed and apologetic. She praised Tara for her kindness. She had not even realized her wallet was missing or that Tara had thrown it to her not at her.

The little girl still felt a bit shaky inside but also quite pleased with the praise being showered on her. She held her head up high. That felt better.

Daddy Helps Mrs. Pogg

"Now, tell me about these kids that ring your door bell and run away," Dad said gently to the old lady.

"It's been happening a lot recently," Mrs. Pogg grumbled. "Sometimes they laugh and shout rude things through the letter box and I get scared."

Dad's lips tightened. "I don't suppose they mean any harm, but I can see it is very upsetting."

"Yes, and it hurts my hip to get up and go to the door."

"That must be tough," he responded. He turned to the children. "Have you kids any idea who is doing it?"

Mel nodded. "It's the boys who've moved into number 12." Dad just nodded.

Ash-ting whispered to Tara. *"Your dad's going to sort it out. I don't think it will happen again."*

Tara kissed Ash-ting's soft furry head.

Then Dad said, "Mrs. Pogg, I don't think you need to worry about that any more." And she smiled a big relieved smile, which made her look so much softer.

Mrs. Pogg Likes Ash-ting

Daddy walked Mrs. Pogg home, and Tara and Ash-ting were allowed to go with them. Of course, when Mrs. Pogg opened her front door she saw her wallet on the floor, where Tara had flung it.

"I'm so sorry," she repeated, and Tara smiled at her and thought she was quite nice really.

Daddy helped the old lady take off her coat. He put the kettle on for a cup of tea because he said she had had a shock, too. Mrs. Pogg found a packet of chocolate cookies, and Tara was allowed to have two, even though it was nearly her bedtime.

Then the old lady showed them some photographs of her daughter and grandchildren, who lived in Australia. She had not seen them for five years, and Tara thought how sad that was.

She felt a buzz in her forehead. Ash-ting said, "Mrs. Pogg doesn't have a computer. Suggest she

comes to your house to talk to her family on Skype, then she can see them all."

So Tara mentioned it to Daddy, who thought it was a splendid idea.

"Mrs. Pogg," he said. "How would you like to come to our house on Sunday? We have a computer and a special free video conference call program called Skype that allows people to see and talk to each other from their computers wherever they are."

"Oh, I would love that!" Mrs. Pogg exclaimed. "We only talk on the phone, and not as often as I would like, as it costs so much."

Mrs. Pogg loved cats, and Tara let her stroke Ash-ting, who purred for her. Tara thought she was very sweet after all.

Dad Visits Number 12

Daddy took Tara home, then said he was just popping over to number 12. "If you're in bed when I get back, I'll draw you that fairy I promised."

Daddy was away for half an hour. He didn't know the family at number 12 because they were new in the street, so he invited them round for a drink on Sunday morning to meet the family and Mrs. Pogg. He said Mrs. Pogg had a bad hip and was very nice but rather lonely.

The new family were delighted to be asked and seemed very friendly. The parents said they were called Margie and Paul. The boys were Blake and Bob.

Dad didn't mention the bell ringing. He knew that if they got to know the old lady, the two boys would not want to taunt her. Blake and Bob looked at Dad strangely when he mentioned the old lady. They wondered if he knew what they had been doing. He thought they looked a bit sheepish.

Sunday Morning

The following Sunday, Daddy used Skype to talk to Mrs. Pogg's family in Australia. Her family already used Skype on their computer, and Mrs. Pogg was amazed at how easy the computer program was to use and overjoyed to see the whole family on the screen. Tara showed everyone in Australia her special kitten and waved his paw to them.

Then the family from number 12 came over. It turned out that Blake and Bob were aged 11 and 12, the same age as Mrs. Pogg's grandsons. "My brother's in Perth, Australia, too," exclaimed Margie, their mother.

So they all went to the computer and once again used Skype to talk to Margie's brother and his family, as well. Margie's brother said it looked as if they had settled into their new home very well and were making friends already. Blake and Bob talked to their cousins, who were just going to bed after a day on the beach! The children were very envious of them, as it was winter in England and very cold.

Later, when it snowed, they all built a snowman for Mrs. Pogg in her front garden, and she gave them an old hat and scarf to put on him. Then Daddy filmed some video of it, and they showed it to their families in Australia via Skype. The cousins in Australia wanted to play in the snow!

And now Mrs. Pogg buys a packet of chocolate cookies every week when she goes shopping, because Tara, Mel, and Jack and their mum often call in to see her. And so do the boys from number 12.

Discussion points and exercises for adults and children

Tara and her Talking Kitten Meet a Mermaid

1. Which archangel is in charge of the ocean kingdom and what colour is he? What do you know about archangels?

2. Why are the sea creatures so angry? Can you think of more reasons than are in the story?

3. Draw an underwater ocean scene and write on it:

   WE WANT CLEAN OCEANS.

4. What did you feel about the helpers eating fish and chips after Tara helped the fish?

5. Close your eyes and imagine you are going on a magical underwater journey to help the sea creatures. What do you experience and how can you assist them?

6. How do you feel about the villagers helping Rocky's family with the threatened flood? Why do you think they all turned out to help?

Tara, Ash-ting and the Wallet

1. Have you ever been unjustly accused of something? How did it feel? What did you do about it? Talk about speaking up for yourself.

2. Discuss ways to sort out problems by being friendly.

3. Life in different parts of the world is different for children. What is good about your country?

4. Do you know anyone who is lonely? How can you make a difference?

5. Draw a snowman, and in the picture put your family and friends and neighbours building it together. You can draw stick people if you want to.

In the same collection... three books

and two audio CDs